Mule School

For Ben and Tom, with love
– J.R.

To Shane
– L.C.

ISBN-13: 0-545-02218-5
ISBN-10: 978-0-545-02218-7

Text copyright © 2007 by Julia Rawlinson
Illustrations copyright © 2007 by Lynne Chapman
All rights reserved. First published in Great Britain by Gullane Children's Books in 2007.

Cover illustration © 2007 by Lynne Chapman

First Scholastic printing, September 2007

Mule
School

Julia Rawlinson

Lynne Chapman

Stomper did not like **Mule School**. He
liked the other mules. He liked lunchtime and playtime.
But he did not like *Stubbornness Practice*.

Every day his schedule was the same:

9 o'clock: **Stubbornness**
11 o'clock: **Kicking**
12 o'clock: **Lunch**
1 o'clock **Stubbornness**
2 o'clock: **Kicking**
3 o'clock: **Home**

Day after day the mules recited "Won't, won't, won't," and "Can't, can't, can't." They **SHOOK** their heads and **STOMPED** their feet.

But one day Stomper put his hoof in the air. "What if we *want* to do as we're told?" he asked nervously.

"You are a mule. Refuse!" cried Mrs. Kick.

"But what if it seems like a good idea?" mumbled Stomper.

"Nobody else's idea is good," she snapped, and sent him to stand in the corner.

Stomper's first
stubbornness test
was to guard a pile of
apples. He stood mumbling,
"No, no, no," under his breath,
but before long a scruffy
pig snuffled up.

"My piglets are hungry. Could you
spare some apples?" she asked.
"Of course." Stomper nodded.
"Help yourself."

The pig waddled happily off with
the apples, but then Stomper gulped.
He had forgotten to be stubborn.

"Fool of a mule," cried Mrs. Kick.
"You must never, ever
give in to a pig."

Stomper's next task
was to block a path.

Soon a family of goats needed to
get past. Stomper stood aside and
waved them by politely.

But then the school's
meanest mules, Biff and Bash,
jumped out and laughed.
"We are mules, we like to kick.
Weakness makes us
sick, sick, sick!"
they chanted as they circled him.

"We're going to tell on you.
You were supposed to stop the
goats, not let them through."

"They're right," thought Stomper sadly. "I am a useless mule."

"Stamp, why am I so weak?"
asked Stomper in the playground.
"You're not weak. You've got a good kick,"
said Stamp. "Come and play ball."

Stamp kicked the ball over the haystack, and Stomper galloped after it, forgetting all his stubbornness troubles as he raced across the playground. They bashed and butted, kicked and crashed until it was time for class.

That afternoon there was a field trip to practice kicking in the valley, but Stomper was sent out apple-picking to replace the apples he had lost.

He wandered up the valley
side, following a butterfly, and was
listening to the mules chanting below
when he heard a frightening sound.

The dam above the valley had...

BUR

ST!

And a huge river was
roaring down. His friends
were going to be . . .

swept away!

"MOVE!"

cried Stomper as loudly
as he could, but the mules
didn't hear him.

"Leaf or branch
or rock or stick,
whatever it is
we'll give it a . . .

kick!"

they chanted,
far below.

"RUN!"

thundered Stomper, waving
his hooves wildly, but
the mules were not looking.

"Nose to the ground
and tail to the sky,
let those thundering
mule hooves . . .

fly!"

they cried as they
kick, kick, kicked.

Then, at last, Mrs. Kick saw the water
swooshing toward her. She faced up the valley,
dug in her hooves, bared her teeth, and cried,

**"We are mules and we won't budge,
even for an . . .**

ENORMOUS FLOOD!"

The other mules took
up the cry. Their eyes
were wide, their ears were
back, but their trembling
hooves were planted
firmly on the ground.

Suddenly, another sound rose above the rushing water.

CRASH! CRASH!

CRASH!

The mules closed their
eyes tightly and covered
their heads with their
hooves, but then . . .

"IT'S STOMPER!"

cried Stamp with a mighty
neigh of delight. Stomper's head was
down, his heels were flying, and he was
kick, kick, kicking with all his might.

CRA

CRASH

CRASH!

CRA

He kicked at rocks, he kicked at
sticks, he kicked at broken branches.
Wood and rocks tumbled down the
valley side with a rumbling roar,
making a new dam that whooshed
the water safely away.

Stomper trotted down the hill and stood, casually nibbling flowers. Slowly, the other mules sidled up. "We were wrong," they muttered, "we were foolish mules."

Stomper shook his head. "No," he said, "you stood your ground. You did what a mule should do. It's just lucky that not all mules are exactly the same as you."

Mrs. Kick looked thoughtful as she led them back to school.

The next day at Mule School the schedule read:

   9 o'clock: **Stubbornness or Pottery**

11 o'clock: **Kicking or Flower Arranging**

12 o'clock: **Lunch**

   1 o'clock: **Stubbornness or Hoof Printing**

   2 o'clock: **Kicking or Musical Mules**

   3 o'clock: **Home**

And at 11 o'clock, while Stomper
happily kicked his way through class . . .

...Biff and Bash were down in the meadow, merrily arranging daisies.